Leona
the Unicorn
Fairy

Special thanks to Narinder Dhami

ISBN 978-0-545-38423-0

12 11 10 9 8 7 6 5 4 3 2 1   12 13 14 15 16/0

Printed in the U.S.A.   40

This edition first printing, March 2012

Leona
the Unicorn
Fairy

by Daisy Meadows

SCHOLASTIC INC.

New York Toronto London Auckland
Sydney Mexico City New Delhi Hong Kong

There are seven special animals,
Who live in Fairyland.
They use their magic powers
To help others where they can.

A dragon, black cat, phoenix,
A seahorse, and snow swan, too,
A unicorn and ice bear—
I know just what to do.

I'll lock them in my castle
And never let them out.
The world will turn more miserable,
Of that, I have no doubt!

Contents

spooked!

"Isn't this great, Kirsty?" Rachel Walker turned around in her saddle to smile at her best friend, Kirsty Tate. "I've only been horseback riding a few times before, but now I just love it!" Then Rachel leaned forward and patted her pony, Sparkle.

"Me, too," agreed Kirsty, who was on a beautiful black pony behind Rachel.

The girls had been taking riding lessons ever since they arrived at camp, but this was the first time they'd been on a trail ride through the forest. "I think it's because Sparkle and Tansy are so sweet. They don't mind if we do something wrong!"

"Keep following the trail, everyone," Susan, their riding instructor, called from the back of the line. There were several other campers on ponies in front of and behind Kirsty and Rachel. "This path will eventually take us back to the camp."

"I can't believe we only have a

day and a half left at camp," Rachel said with a sigh as the ponies ambled through the forest. It was cool and shady under the trees, but beams of sunlight dappled the grass here and there. "We've had such a good time, haven't we, Kirsty? We've tried hiking, orienteering, and bird-watching, and we've made some great friends."

But Kirsty wasn't really listening. She was looking around, peeking through the trees on either side of the trail.

"Sorry, Rachel," she said quickly. "I was just seeing if I could spot anything unusual."

Rachel smiled. She knew exactly what Kirsty was looking for! On the day the girls arrived at camp, the king and queen of Fairyland had asked for their help. Kirsty and Rachel had discovered that Jack Frost and his goblins had kidnapped

seven young magical
animals from the
Magical Animal
Fairies. These animals
had the power to
spread the kind of
magic qualities that every

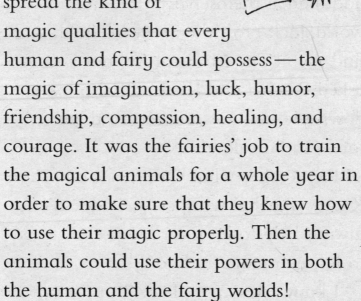

human and fairy could possess—the
magic of imagination, luck, humor,
friendship, compassion, healing, and
courage. It was the fairies' job to train
the magical animals for a whole year in
order to make sure that they knew how
to use their magic properly. Then the
animals could use their powers in both
the human and the fairy worlds!

But Jack Frost was determined to
disrupt the magical animals' training.
He didn't want *anyone*, humans or

fairies, to be happy. So, with the help of his goblins, Jack Frost had stolen the animals from Fairyland and imprisoned them in his Ice Castle! But the young animals had managed to escape and had hidden themselves in the human world. Jack Frost then sent his goblins to find them! The Magical Animal Fairies asked Rachel and Kirsty to help track down the animals and return them safely to Fairyland.

"Remember what Queen Titania says, Kirsty," Rachel whispered. "It doesn't always help to look for magic. You need to let the magic find you!"

"I know," Kirsty replied. "But it's so hard! I just want to find Leona's unicorn and Caitlin's ice bear. I'm worried about them, because they haven't learned how to use their magic powers properly yet."

"We're doing OK, though," Rachel pointed out. "We've already found Ashley's dragon, Lara's little black cat, Erin's phoenix, Rihanna's seahorse, and Sophia's snow swan."

"That's true," Kirsty said with a smile. "Let's just enjoy the trail ride and wait for the magic to come to us!"

Rachel nodded. "Look, Kirsty, there's another fox," she said, catching a glimpse of something brown between the trees. "That makes two that we've seen now."

"Yes, plus three rabbits and six squirrels!" Kirsty replied. "There's a lot of wildlife around here, isn't there?"

Suddenly, without any warning at all, the pony in front of Rachel and Kirsty gave a frightened neigh and reared up. Lauren, the camper riding the pony, gasped with fright.

"Quick, Rachel!" Kirsty cried urgently, spotting a side path to her left. "Over here!"

Swiftly, Kirsty and Rachel pulled Tansy and Sparkle off the trail and down the side path to avoid a collision. Meanwhile, Lauren got her pony, Sky, under control again.

"Are you all right, girls?" called Susan, trotting toward them. "Looks like Sky was spooked by something."

"I'm fine," said Lauren, patting Sky's neck. Rachel and Kirsty nodded in agreement.

"Good thinking, you two," Susan went on, smiling at them. "You got your ponies out of the way just in time."

As the riders moved on again, Kirsty and Rachel turned their ponies around so they could rejoin the others on the main path. Just then, Kirsty saw a sudden flash of bright green in the undergrowth around her. She immediately turned to her friend.

"Rachel!" Kirsty gasped. "I just saw something green—and it wasn't leafy!"

"Do you think it was a goblin?" Rachel whispered, alarmed. "Maybe there's more wildlife in this forest than we thought!"

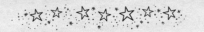

"It could have been a goblin that scared Lauren's pony," Kirsty suggested.

"We'll check it out," Rachel said. "Let's hang back so we're at the end of the line."

The girls waited until the other campers had ridden past, then they trotted back onto the trail some distance behind them. They kept a sharp lookout for goblins, but didn't see anything.

Then Rachel heard a rustling in the bushes. Before she could say anything to Kirsty, two goblins jumped out onto the path— right in front of them!

The Unicorn Appears

"Oh!" Kirsty gasped, quickly bringing
Tansy to a halt. Rachel did the same
with Sparkle.

The biggest goblin nudged the smaller
one and pointed at the two ponies.

"Is one of those a unicorn?" he
whispered in a loud voice.

Rachel glanced at Kirsty. They knew the
goblins must be looking for Leona's unicorn,
one of the missing magical animals!

The smallest goblin looked disgusted. "Are you crazy?" he demanded. "These are ponies, not unicorns! Unicorns have a horn on top of their heads—"

"Don't call me crazy!" the other goblin screeched.

"Well, you *are*!" the smallest goblin yelled. "Whoever heard of a unicorn without a horn?"

Arguing loudly, the two goblins began pushing each other. Kirsty was worried. The path was too narrow to get past the fighting goblins, and the goblins were getting

closer to the girls and their ponies.

"Look out!" Kirsty called.

The biggest goblin pushed the smaller
one in front of Rachel's pony. Sparkle
gave a loud, startled neigh and reared up.
The goblins yelped in alarm and ran off
through the undergrowth.

"It's OK, Sparkle!" Rachel said uncertainly, trying to get the frightened pony under control. But Sparkle bolted off at top speed through the trees, with Rachel clinging desperately to the reins.

"Oh, no!" Kirsty cried, horrified. "Hold on, Rachel!" Kirsty urged Tansy to follow them.

Rachel's heart was pounding as Sparkle galloped

through the forest. She had to keep ducking to avoid low branches, and she was very worried that she'd fall off the pony or get hit by a branch.

"Whoa, Sparkle!" she called. Remembering what they'd been taught

in their riding lessons, Rachel squeezed
Sparkle's sides with her legs and pulled
back on the reins. Unfortunately, Sparkle
slowed down and stopped too quickly.
Rachel wasn't expecting that, and she
flew right over the pony's head.

"Rachel!" Kirsty shouted, riding up
behind Sparkle just in time to see her
friend go sailing through the air.

To Kirsty's relief, she saw that Rachel had landed on a soft, springy patch of moss on the forest floor. Jumping quickly down from Tansy's back, Kirsty rushed over to her friend.

"Are you OK, Rachel?" Kirsty asked, kneeling down beside her. She could see that Rachel was holding her arm, looking shaken.

"I'm fine, except I think I sprained my wrist," Rachel replied, wincing. "It hurts a lot."

"I'll run and find Susan to get help," Kirsty said, glancing around. "They couldn't have made it much farther up the trail."

But at that moment, Kirsty saw a gleam of pure, dazzling white shining through the trees. It appeared to be

coming straight toward them!

"Rachel, look!" Kirsty exclaimed with wonder as the white shape came closer. "It's a unicorn."

"It's Leona's missing magical animal!" Rachel whispered, her eyes wide.

The beautiful young unicorn came trotting through the trees toward them. He was about the size of a Shetland pony, and his coat was gleaming white. He had gold hooves, and a twisted golden horn on his head.

The unicorn stopped several feet from

Rachel and Kirsty. He lowered his snow-
white head, shaking his long mane.
Suddenly,
a shower of gold glitter
burst from his horn.
It flew through
the air and
circled
Rachel's
injured wrist
like a
bracelet.

The girls
could hardly
believe their eyes.
A few seconds later, the glitter began to
disappear in a sparkling mist.

"Rachel! Kirsty! Where are you?"

"That's Susan," Kirsty said as they

heard the sound of a horse's hooves. "She's looking for us."

The unicorn's ears pricked up. Quickly, he turned and galloped off through the trees.

"Oh, please come back!" Rachel called after him. She turned to Kirsty, looking worried. "How will we ever find him again, Kirsty?"

"I don't know." Kirsty frowned. "Let's just hope the goblins don't find him first!"

Leona's Lollipop

Kirsty reached out her hand to help
Rachel to her feet. As she stood up,
Rachel gasped suddenly.

"Does your wrist hurt?" Kirsty asked
sympathetically.

Rachel shook her head. "No, that's just
it," she replied, bending her wrist back
and forth. "It's all better!"

"I just remembered," Kirsty said
excitedly. "The unicorn's magic power is
healing. He must have healed your wrist
with the glitter from his horn!"

At that moment,
Susan rode toward
them through the
trees.

"Are you OK,
girls?" she asked,
dismounting
quickly and
coming over.
"We just realized
that you weren't
with us on the
trail."

"Sparkle got
spooked and

bolted," Rachel explained. She hoped
the goblins weren't anywhere around.
It would be a disaster if Susan spotted
them, because no one was supposed to
know that Fairyland existed! "But I'm
fine."

"It's lucky you were wearing your
riding helmet, or you could have been
really hurt," Susan said, as she checked
Rachel over.

Rachel winked
at Kirsty. "Luck
and the healing
touch of a
unicorn!" she
whispered, as Susan
checked Sparkle for
injuries, too.

"OK, time to get back to camp," Susan

said briskly. "I think you've had enough excitement for one day, and your free-time block is coming up. You don't want to miss that!"

Reluctantly, Rachel and Kirsty climbed back onto their ponies.

"I don't want to leave the unicorn in the forest all alone," Kirsty said to Rachel as they followed Susan back to the trail. "Not with the goblins around!"

"Let's come back and search for the unicorn after we've put Sparkle and

Tansy in the stables," Rachel suggested.

Back at the camp, Rachel and Kirsty led the ponies into their shared stall and carefully began to brush them. The stable door was open and, as Rachel and Kirsty brushed their ponies' manes, they heard voices outside.

"Do you know if any ponies have escaped from the stables, Katie?" someone asked. Kirsty and Rachel recognized the voice. It was Emma, one of their bunkmates. "I think I saw a small white pony heading toward the amphitheater just now."

"Really? You must be seeing things!" Katie said teasingly. "We don't have any white ponies at the camp."

Kirsty and Rachel glanced at each other in alarm. So the unicorn *had* come to the camp! The amphitheater was a round, open-air theater where the campers could put on shows and perform

plays, and it wasn't far from the stables.

"That's what I thought." Emma sounded puzzled. "What's *really* weird is that it looked like the pony had a twisted horn on its head!"

"Maybe it's a unicorn?" Katie suggested, laughing.

Emma laughed, too. "It's probably just a practical joke," she said. "The campers and counselors have been playing funny tricks on one another all week, right? I found a plastic frog inside one of my rain boots this morning!"

Rachel turned to Kirsty as the other two girls walked away, still laughing.

"I think the unicorn must have followed us back to camp!" Rachel exclaimed. "We have to find him before someone realizes he's a *real* unicorn."

"Or before he's captured by the goblins," Kirsty added.

Quickly, Rachel and Kirsty gave Tansy and Sparkle their buckets of grain, plus a few carrots for a treat. Then they rushed out of the stall.

"Rachel?" Susan popped out of one of the other stalls as they went by. "I want you to stop by the first-aid cabin and see Elizabeth, the camp nurse."

"But I'm fine," Rachel insisted.

"It can't hurt to be sure, can it?" Susan said kindly. "Off you go."

Rachel frowned as Susan went back into the stall.

"I hope this doesn't take too long," she said anxiously as she and Kirsty hurried to the first-aid cabin.

"Ah, there you are, Rachel." Elizabeth

was at her desk rolling up bandages
when the girls knocked and went in.
She was young and friendly, with a
snow-white uniform and long red hair
neatly pinned back. "Let's take a look
at you. Any bumps or bruises?"

Rachel shook her head.

"Well, you seem fine," Elizabeth remarked a few minutes later with a smile. "I think you can safely go and enjoy the rest of the afternoon."

"Thanks, Elizabeth," Rachel said, jumping eagerly to her feet. "Sorry to have wasted your time."

"Oh, it was nice to have something to do," Elizabeth replied. "I usually see a dozen or more campers every day with various bumps and bruises, but you're the only ones I've seen so far today." She picked up another roll of bandages. "So I decided to organize my medicine cabinet instead."

"That's because of Leona's unicorn,"

Kirsty whispered to Rachel as they went to the door of the cabin. "His healing powers mean that the campers don't need the nurse!"

"Help yourself to a lollipop from my jar on your way out, girls," Elizabeth called.

There was a big glass jar of brightly colored lollipops on a shelf near the door. As Rachel reached for it, she noticed that the jar had a strange glow.

"What's going on?" Rachel whispered to Kirsty. Her eyes were wide with amazement

as she unscrewed the lid.

Kirsty looked excited. She put her hand into the jar and pulled out a red strawberry-flavored lollipop. Clinging to the top of it was a tiny fairy!

Twisty on the Loose

Kirsty nearly cried out in surprise. She and Rachel smiled down at the fairy, who wore wide-legged blue pants, a matching sweater, and a starry gold belt. Her long blond hair was tied up in a ponytail.

"Hello, girls!" the fairy called quietly, her eyes twinkling. "I'm so glad I found

you! Remember me? I'm Leona the
Unicorn Fairy."

"Hi, Leona," Rachel and Kirsty
whispered back.

Quickly the girls left the first-aid cabin
with Kirsty carrying the
lollipop.

"As you know,
I'm looking for
my unicorn, Twisty,"
Leona explained. "I
thought he might be
attracted to the first-aid
cabin because he has
special healing
powers." She looked
anxiously at
Rachel and Kirsty.
"Have you seen him?"

"Yes, but not here," Rachel told Leona. She quickly explained how Twisty had appeared in the forest and healed her injured wrist.

"But now we think Twisty is right here in the camp!" Kirsty added. "Emma, our bunkmate, saw him near the amphitheater. But don't worry, Leona, she thought it was some sort of joke."

Leona looked relieved. "We'd better get to the amphitheater right away!" she said. She dived into Kirsty's pocket out of sight, and the girls hurried off.

The amphitheater was at the edge of camp. As they approached it, Rachel blinked several

times in surprise. She could see human-
sized fairies dancing around the stage,
wearing flowy white dresses and gauzy
wings on their shoulders.

"They're not *real* fairies, Rachel," Kirsty
said with a grin. "They're just campers in
costume! Look, one of them is Catherine,
from our cabin."

"You're right," Rachel agreed. "For a minute there, I thought we had some visitors from Fairyland!"

A fairy king and queen, wearing golden crowns, were also dancing among the fairies. As the girls got closer to the stage, Kirsty did a double take. Was that a *goblin* skipping along next to the fairy queen? But when Kirsty looked again, there was no one there.

I've got goblins on the brain! Kirsty thought, shaking her head.

"Hey, Katrina," Rachel called to a camper who was watching the dancers. "What's going on?"

"Oh, this is a rehearsal for Shakespeare's play *A Midsummer Night's Dream*," Katrina explained.

At that moment another camper named Tom wandered by. He heard what Katrina was saying and looked confused.

"Hey, Katrina, there isn't a unicorn in the play, is there?" he asked.

Rachel and Kirsty exchanged glances as Katrina shook her head.

"No, why?"

Tom laughed. "Someone must have attached a horn to a Shetland pony's head as a joke, then!" he replied. "I just saw it leave the amphitheater and trot toward the clubhouse."

"Well, there aren't supposed to be any goblins in this play, either." Katrina shrugged. "But I've seen two campers dressed up as goblins this afternoon!"

Rachel and Kirsty both gasped. So the goblins were at the camp, too!

"I even overheard one of the actors refuse to take off his goblin costume," Katrina said with a laugh. "Some people really get into their parts!"

"We'd better go straight to the clubhouse," Leona whispered, peeking her head out of Kirsty's pocket as the girls hurried off. "The goblins are on Twisty's trail, too. We have to find him before they do!"

Rachel and Kirsty ran to the clubhouse. They took a quick look around outside, but didn't see Twisty.

"What are we going to do, Rachel?" Kirsty asked desperately. "We can't run around the camp all day!"

"Let's ask inside if anyone's seen anything," Rachel suggested.

The girls rushed into the clubhouse. Some of the campers were playing Ping-Pong and pool, while others were watching a movie on TV.

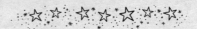

Rachel went over to the boys playing pool. "Sorry to bother you," she said, "but have you seen a pony dressed up like a unicorn today?"

"I did," said one of the boys. "When I was playing football."

"What happened?" Rachel asked eagerly.

"Well, I fell and skinned my knees," the boy explained. "When I came off the field, the pony was standing there watching me. Then it shook its mane and glitter fell all over me!" The boy laughed. "I guess someone was trying to trick me into thinking it was a magic unicorn!"

Kirsty and Rachel glanced down at the boy's knees. They didn't look badly cut at all.

"Maybe the unicorn helped heal the boy, just like he did for you, Rachel," Kirsty whispered.

"I saw the pretend unicorn down by

the dock at the lake," another boy at the pool table added. "It looks really real! I tried to get a closer look, but he trotted away."

Rachel and Kirsty hurried out of the clubhouse.

"So Twisty could be in *two* places," Rachel said as Leona popped out of Kirsty's pocket. "The sports fields or the lake."

"If we choose the wrong one, we might miss him," Leona pointed out.

"Maybe we should split up," suggested Kirsty. "Leona could go to the lake, because it's farther away and flying will be quicker. Rachel and I can search the sports fields."

Leona nodded. "Good thinking, Kirsty," she said. "I'll meet you back at the stables in fifteen minutes."

Then Leona rose up into the air and zoomed away, her blond hair flying.

"I don't like being away from Leona, but we have to find Twisty before someone realizes he's a real unicorn," Rachel said with a sigh, as she and Kirsty dashed off.

"Or before the goblins find him!" Kirsty added.

The girls raced to the sports fields and began to look around carefully. But to their disappointment, Twisty wasn't there.

"What now?" Rachel asked.

"I guess we'd better head back to the stables to meet Leona," Kirsty began, but she stopped when a flash of white in the nearby woods caught her eye.

"Rachel!" Kirsty cried. "It's Twisty!"

A Ransom Note

"Careful!" Rachel whispered. She gazed at the unicorn grazing on the grass between the trees. "We shouldn't frighten him."

The girls sneaked across the field toward the unicorn. As they tiptoed up to him, Rachel wondered how they could catch him and take him back to Leona. Suddenly, she realized she still had a

carrot in her pocket from feeding the
ponies earlier. She took it out and showed
it silently to Kirsty, who nodded.

"Here, Twisty," Rachel called, holding
the carrot in front of the unicorn's nose.

Twisty raised
his head and
sniffed the
carrot. Rachel
moved away
a little, and
the unicorn
walked after
her, his beautiful
dark eyes fixed
on the carrot just
in front of him.

Rachel led Twisty through the forest,
then took a back route toward the stables

so that they would be less likely to bump
into other campers. Kirsty went in front,
keeping a sharp lookout to make sure no
one else was around.

When they reached the stables, both
girls sighed with relief. They patted
Twisty, who shook his mane and gave a
little neigh.

"Thank you for healing my wrist
today, Twisty," Rachel said, feeding him
the carrot.

"I wonder where Leona is," Kirsty
said with a frown, glancing around as
Twisty crunched on his carrot. Suddenly,
she spotted a piece of paper stuck to
the door of the stables. "What's that,
Rachel?"

"It looks like a note," Rachel replied.
"What does it say?"

The note was in shaky handwriting
in green ink. It read:

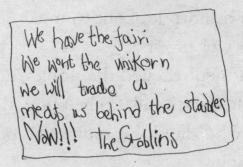

"I don't believe it!" Rachel cried. "The
goblins aren't smart enough to catch
Leona."

"Or *any* fairy!" Kirsty agreed. "It might
be a trap. But we'd better go and meet
them, just in case."

Quickly, the girls led Twisty around
the back of the stables. They held on
tightly to the unicorn, afraid that the
goblins might try to pounce on him and
steal him.

The two goblins who'd
spooked Sparkle in the
forest earlier were
standing by the
ponies' water trough.
The small one was
holding Nurse
Elizabeth's lollipop
jar. As Rachel, Kirsty,

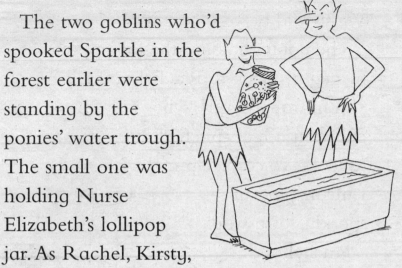

and Twisty came closer, the goblin shook
the jar. It sparkled in the sun like magic
fairy dust.

"Oh, no!" Rachel whispered to Kirsty.
"Maybe the goblins *did* capture Leona in
that big jar!"

But Kirsty shook her head. "No,
Leona would use her magic to
escape," she replied. "It could just be
something else sparkling inside the jar.

We should be very careful!"

The goblin holding the lollipop jar turned his back to Rachel and Kirsty.

"I'm trapped, girls!" he called in a high-pitched, squeaky voice. "Help me! I mean, *please* in a sparkly, fairy way!"

Rachel and Kirsty tried not to laugh. It was really obvious that the goblin was only pretending to have Leona in that jar!

"Hand over the unicorn!" the other goblin demanded, stepping forward, "and we'll let your fairy friend go."

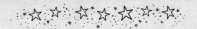

At that moment, Rachel and Kirsty noticed a twinkling light zipping through the air toward the goblins. It was Leona! Now the girls knew the goblins were bluffing.

"We know you don't have Leona," Rachel said firmly.

"We *do* have her!" The goblin stomped his foot in a rage. "We captured her when she was flying toward the lake."

"And we know she's not with you," the goblin with the jar said triumphantly, "or the unicorn wouldn't still be here!"

"But *we* know where Leona is," Kirsty said. She and Rachel both pointed above the goblins' heads.

"Don't try to trick us!" the goblin with the jar insisted. "We've been fooled by you before. Now, give us the unicorn!"

Ponies to the Rescue

Suddenly, Leona swooped down, giving the goblins a cheery wave. They shrieked with surprise.

"Get her!" the bigger goblin roared.

Quickly, the other goblin unscrewed the jar. He pulled out a handful of glitter and tossed it at Leona. The fairy had to dart around and dodge the sparkles.

"We have to help Leona!" Kirsty cried. "Keep hold of Twisty, Rachel!"

Rachel nodded. Immediately, Kirsty dashed forward. She had to distract the goblin somehow. As the goblin threw another shower of sparkles at Leona, Kirsty rushed over to Tansy's and Sparkle's stall.

"Tansy, Sparkle!" she called.

When the ponies saw Kirsty, they immediately stuck their heads out of the open top of the door, hoping to be pet. They neighed happily—and the goblins almost jumped out of their skins!

"Help!" shouted the bigger goblin with terror. "It's those scary ponies again!"

The smaller goblin also gave a yell of surprise. He dropped the lollipop jar, spilling glitter on the ground. Kirsty quickly grabbed the jar.

But as Leona headed toward Twisty, the bigger goblin made one last attempt to catch her. He took a giant leap. Luckily, Leona slipped through his fingers! The goblin sailed through the air and landed with a thud in a pile of horse manure.

"Yuck, gross!" said the smaller goblin with a snicker.

"Here, Twisty!" Leona called, holding out her arms as she flew toward the unicorn.

Smiling, Rachel released Twisty. He cantered up and bounded through the air to Leona. As he did, he shrank down to his tiny fairy-size again.

"It's so good to see you again, Twisty!" Leona declared, giving him a hug. Then she jumped onto his back. They zoomed up and out of the reach of the smaller goblin, who stood staring up at them sulkily.

"Oh, my ankle hurts!" the goblin on the ground moaned.

Twisty immediately
circled in the air
and hovered over
the goblin. A
shower of glitter
burst from the
unicorn's golden

horn and whirled around the goblin's
injured ankle.

"It's all better!" the goblin said in
amazement, jumping to his feet. Looking
sheepish, he glanced up at Leona and
Twisty. "Thanks," he mumbled.

"Come on, let's go," the smaller goblin
snapped. "I'm fed up with pesky fairies
and silly girls who ruin all our plans!"

"Me, too," the other goblin agreed as
they stomped off.

"Girls, you've done it again!" Leona

said happily. "Because of you, almost all our magical animals are safely back in Fairyland and can start their training again. We can never thank you enough — but thank you, anyway!"

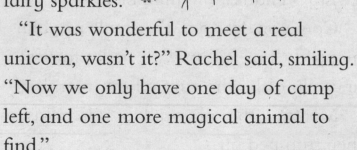

"Good-bye," the girls called as Leona and Twisty disappeared in a burst of fairy sparkles.

"It was wonderful to meet a real unicorn, wasn't it?" Rachel said, smiling. "Now we only have one day of camp left, and one more magical animal to find."

"Yes, Caitlin's ice bear," Kirsty replied.

"But that's a problem. The ice bear's special power is courage." She looked solemnly at Rachel. "So, while she's missing, will we be able to find the courage to take on the goblins?"

THE MAGICAL ANIMAL FAIRIES

Leona the Unicorn Fairy has taken
her magical animal back to Fairyland!
Now Rachel and Kirsty need to help . . .

Caitlin
the Ice Bear Fairy!

Join their next adventure
in this special sneak peek. . . .

Frosty Sparkles!

"I can't believe it's the last day of camp already," Kirsty Tate said sadly as she finished packing her bag and zipped it shut. She gazed around the cozy wooden cabin where she and her best friend, Rachel Walker, had spent the week with four other girls. They'd been staying at an adventure camp and had taken part in all kinds of activities—exploring caves, canoeing, horseback riding . . . plus making some very special fairy friends!

The week of camp was almost over now, and their bunkmates had packed their things and were ready to go home. Only Kirsty and Rachel were left in the cabin.

"We've had such amazing adventures this week," Rachel said, smiling as she thought about them.

Kirsty put on her jacket. "Well, our time here isn't over yet," she reminded Rachel. "We're still going to climb High Hill . . . and we've got to rescue the last magical animal, too."

Rachel nodded, an anxious expression appearing on her face. "Oh, I hope we find the little ice bear," she said. "I hate thinking about her being lost and alone."

"Or caught by Jack Frost's goblins," Kirsty added, frowning. "We can't let that happen."

It was kind of cold outside, so Rachel grabbed their hats and scarves. "Come on," she said. "The sooner we get out there and start looking, the better!"

No one else at camp knew it, but Kirsty and Rachel had been having some extra-special adventures . . . helping the Magical Animal Fairies find their missing animals! Jack Frost had stolen them, but the clever animals had found a way to escape from his Ice Castle and enter the human world, where they'd been lost ever since. So far, the two girls had helped the fairies track down a baby dragon, a magic black cat, a young phoenix, a seahorse, snow swan, and unicorn. But they still needed to find the ice bear cub. . . .

RAINBOW magic

These activities are magical!
Play dress-up, send friendship notes, and much more!

SCHOLASTIC
www.scholastic.com
www.rainbowmagiconline.com

HIT entertainment

RMACTIV3